DATE DUE

MR 2'91	DEC 14	JN 17 '22	
JY 22'91	AUG 30 '96		
JY 13'92	AUG 28 97		
MY 10'93	JY 0 2		
SE 19	JY 12 01		
NOV 29 '93	AG 15 02		
DEC 28 '93	JE 17 03		
FEB 17 '94	AP 22 04		
FEB 17 '94	SE 0 5		
MAY 28 '94	NV 0 2		
FEB 14 '95			
APR 13 '95	AG 2 5		

DEMCO

Richard Scarry's
Lowly Worm Storybook

A Random House PICTUREBACK®

Richard Scarry's

Lowly Worm
Storybook

The Library of Congress has cataloged the first printing of this title as follows: Scarry, Richard. Richard Scarry's Lowly worm storybook—New York: Random House, c1977. (A Random House pictureback) (The Best book club ever) SUMMARY: Presents five brief stories in which the baker makes a loaf of talking bread, Mr. Fixit is finally stumped, Mr. Rabbit learns the consequences of absent-mindedness, three sitters make fudge, and Tanglefoot takes a spill. [1. Animals—Fiction. 2. Short stories] I. Title. II. Title: Lowly worm storybook. PZ7.S327Rl [E] 77-79842 ISBN: 0-394-83706-1 (B.C.); 0-394-88270-9 (trade)

Manufactured in the United States of America 1 2 3 4 5 6 7 8 9 0

77803

RANDOM HOUSE NEW YORK

THE TALKING BREAD

Humperdink, the baker, was mixing bread
dough with the help of Able Baker Charlie
Mouse. Humperdink's little girl, Flossie,
watched them squish and squash the dough.

After they had kneaded the dough by squishing and
squashing, they patted it into loaves of all different
shapes and sizes.

Then Humperdink put the loaves into the hot oven to bake.

After they had finished baking, he set them out on the
table to cool. M-m-m-m-m! Fresh bread smells good!

Mamma!

LISTEN! Did you hear that? When Humperdink took out the last loaf, it said, "Mamma." But everybody knows that bread can't talk. THAT LOAF MUST BE HAUNTED!

"HELP! POLICE!"
Humperdink picked up Flossie and ran from the room.
"I must telephone Sergeant Murphy," he said.

Sergeant Murphy arrived in a hurry.

Mamma!

He reached down and picked up the loaf
of haunted bread.

"Mamma!" the bread said.

Murphy was so startled he
fell into the mixing trough.

At just that moment, Huckle and
Lowly came into the bakery.
"That is a *very* strange loaf of
bread," said Lowly. Stretching out,
he slowly ooched toward it.

He took a nibble.
The bread said nothing.

He nibbled and nibbled until
only his foot was showing . . .
and still the bread said nothing.

Mamma!

Lowly stood up. Once again
the bread said, "Mamma!"
    Finally Lowly stuck
out his head. "I have solved
the mystery," he said. "Break
the loaf open, but *please*
. . . don't break me!"

Humperdink gently broke open
the bread and inside was
. . . Flossie's talking DOLL.
It had fallen into the mixing
trough and been baked
inside the bread.
    With the mystery solved,
they all sat down to eat
the haunted bread. All except
Lowly, that is. He had already
eaten his fill.

Mamma!

Baby!

All right, Lowly! Please take
your foot off the table!

MR. FIXIT

Mr. Fixit can fix ANYTHING.
At least that is what he once told me.

He fixed the wheel on Philip's wagon.

He fixed the flat tire
on the school bus.
Don't you think that you
should stop now, Mr. Fixit?

He fixed Mrs. Pussycat's automobile.

He also fixed Sam's boat so that it wouldn't ever leak again. My, that was a leaky boat!

Dadda!

Mary's talking doll couldn't
say "Mamma" anymore.
Mr. Fixit fixed it.
Now it says "Dadda."

He fixed Mother Cat's
vacuum cleaner, but he
made a little mistake.
It won't vacuum
the floor anymore.

Mr. Fixit told Mother Cat
she was lucky to be the only
one with a vacuum cleaner
like that!

When he fixed Lowly Worm's shoe,
Lowly said, "You are a genius.
I'll bet there isn't anything
you can't fix."

"You are right, Lowly," said
Mr. Fixit. "I can fix anything!"

Then Mr. Fixit went home. After his wife kissed him, she said,
"Will you please give Little Fixit his bottle while I am cooking supper?"

Mr. Fixit filled the baby bottle with milk. BUT . . .
he didn't know how to fix the nipple on the top.

He tried and he tried, but he couldn't
get it on. What a mess he was making!

Little Fixit said, "Daddy, let me try."
"It *can't* be done," said Mr. Fixit.
But he let Little Fixit try anyhow.
And Little Fixit fixed it—
on the very first try!

"WHY, THAT'S AMAZING!"
said Mr. Fixit. "Show *me* how to do it."
Now, just be patient, Mr. Fixit.
Let him finish his bottle first and
then he will show you how.

ABSENT-MINDED MR. RABBIT

Mr. Rabbit walked down the street. He wasn't looking at
the workmen, who were making a new, hot, sticky, gooey street.
No! He was looking at his newspaper.

He wasn't looking at his feet,
which were getting sticky and gooey, too.
No! He was looking at his newspaper.

Then suddenly he stopped looking at his newspaper.
He looked down at his feet instead. And do you know what he saw?
He saw that he was STUCK in that new, hot, sticky, gooey street!

The workmen got a long pole and tried
to poke him out. It didn't work.

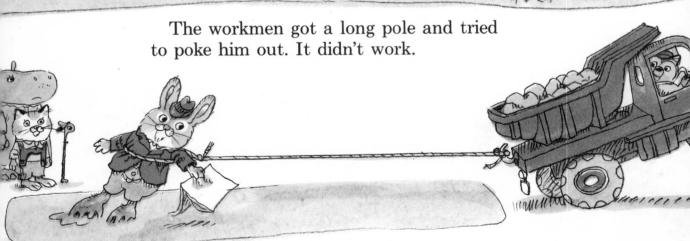

A truck tried to pull him out with a rope. No good! He was stuck all right!

They tried to blow him out with a huge fan.
The fan blew off his hat and coat . . .
but Mr. Rabbit remained stuck.

Some firemen tried to squirt him out.
They squirted water at his shirt and necktie—
but Mr. Rabbit remained stuck. REALLY STUCK!
Well, now! He can't stay there forever!
Somebody has to think of a way to get him out.

Aha! Here comes a power shovel!
Let's see what it will try to do.

Well, the power shovel reached down . . .
and scooped up Mr. Rabbit.

It dropped him gently to the dry ground.
He would certainly have to wash his feet when he
got home. But at least he was no longer stuck.

He put on his clothes and thanked everyone.
As he was leaving, he promised that after this
he would always look where he was going.

But a little while later, Mr. Rabbit
was reading his newspaper again. He had
forgotten his promise. And, naturally,
he wasn't watching where he was going.

UH-OH! DON'T LOOK!!

Mother Bear saw Wolfgang, Benny, and Harry walking by. She ran out and said, "My house is a mess. I've got to clean it from top to bottom. Will you please baby-sit with Robert while I go shopping for some soap?"

Wolfgang, Benny, and Harry all agreed to stay and play with Robert while Mother Bear was shopping.

After a while they got tired of playing.

"I have a good idea," said Harry. "Let's make some fudge."

(I don't think Mother Bear would approve of that, do you?)

When they had finished mixing everything together they poured it into a pan. (Do you suppose they *really* know how to make fudge?)

Then they all sat down at the kitchen
table to wait for the fudge to cook.
Gurgle, burble! Burble, gurgle!
Something seems to be bubbling over!

POP!!!!
The oven door burst open.
The fudge had exploded!
RUN! RUN FOR YOUR LIVES!

Lowly ran to the telephone.
"HELP!" he cried.
"The fudge is rising!
Our house is sinking in fudge!"

Look out, everyone!
Here come the firemen now. My, they are quick.

But, Lowly, WAIT!
Don't turn on the water hydrant until the firemen attach the big hose to it.

Soon every bit of fudge had been washed out
of the house—along with a few other things.
But LOOK! Who is that coming?
Why, it's Mother Bear. Hurry up, fellows!
Straighten the house before she gets home.
Put everything back in place.
   And hurry up they did!

"I have never seen my house looking so spick-and-span," said Mother Bear. "I think we should have a party. Who would like to make some fudge?"

Lowly spoke right up. "I think it would be better if you made it, Mother Bear."

And so she did. And everyone ate the best fudge in the cleanest, spick-est, span-est house ever!

TANGLEFOOT

Tanglefoot was going to the supermarket to buy a can of soup for his mother. She told him to be careful not to trip and fall.

"I never trip and fall," said Tanglefoot.

But he tripped and fell out the front door.

He tumbled over a baby carriage.

Then he fell into
the supermarket.

He bumped into the grocer.

He knocked over the butcher.

He tripped . . . and cans of
soup went flying all over.

O-O-O-F! Big Hilda was in his way.

"I must stop tripping
and falling," Tanglefoot
said to himself.

But then he fell over
the check-out counter.

He walked home without tripping
once. Very good, Tanglefoot!

He even helped his mother make
a big pot of soup for supper.

But when she poured it into a
big bowl, he fell into it!

Tanglefoot said, "I don't think
I can trip and fall once more today."

But he did!

Good night, Tanglefoot.
Sleep tight.